Sam, Bangs & Moonshine

SAM, BANGS
&
MOONSHINE

written and illustrated by
EVALINE NESS

Holt, Rinehart and Winston
New York   Chicago   San Francisco

Sam, Bangs & Moonshine

On a small island, near a large harbor, there once lived a fisherman's little daughter (named Samantha, but always called Sam), who had the reckless habit of lying.

Not even the sailors home from the sea could tell stranger stories than Sam. Not even the ships in the harbor, with curious cargoes from giraffes to gerbils, claimed more wonders than Sam did.

Sam said her mother was a mermaid, when everyone knew she was dead.

Sam said she had a fierce lion at home, and a baby kangaroo. (Actually, what she *really* had was an old wise cat called Bangs.)

Sam even said that Bangs could talk if and when he wanted to.

Sam said this. Sam said that. But whatever Sam said you could never believe.

Even Bangs yawned and shook his head when she said the ragged old rug on the doorstep was a chariot drawn by dragons.

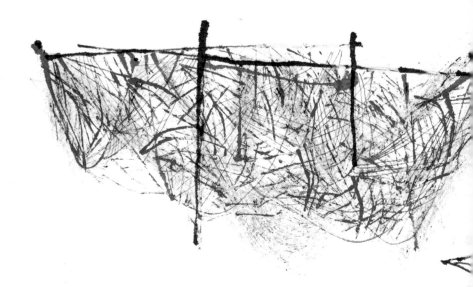

Early one morning, before Sam's father left in his fishing boat to be gone all day, he hugged Sam hard and said, "Today, for a change, talk REAL not MOONSHINE. MOONSHINE spells trouble."

Sam promised. But while she washed the dishes, made the beds, and swept the floor, she wondered what he meant. When she asked Bangs to explain REAL and MOONSHINE, Bangs jumped on her shoulder and purred, "MOONSHINE is flumma-diddle. REAL is the opposite."

Sam decided that Bangs made no sense whatever.

When the sun made a golden star on the cracked window, Sam knew it was time to expect Thomas.

Thomas lived in the tall grand house on the hill. Thomas had two cows in the barn, twenty-five sheep, a bicycle with a basket, and a jungle-gym on the lawn. But most important of all, Thomas believed every word Sam said.

At the same time every day Thomas rode his bicycle down the hill to Sam's house and begged to see her baby kangaroo.

Every day Sam told Thomas it had just "stepped out." She sent Thomas everywhere to find it. She sent him to the tallest trees where, she said, it was visiting owls. Or perhaps it was up in the old windmill, grinding corn for its evening meal.

"It might be," said Sam, "in the lighthouse tower, warning ships at sea."

"Or maybe," she said, "it's asleep on the sand. Somewhere, anywhere on the beach."

Wherever Sam sent Thomas, he went. He climbed up trees, ran down steps, and scoured the beach, but he never found Sam's baby kangaroo.

While Thomas searched, Sam sat in her chariot and was drawn by dragons to faraway secret worlds.

Today, when Thomas arrived, Sam said, "That baby kangaroo just left to visit my mermaid mother. She lives in a cave behind Blue Rock."

Sam watched Thomas race away on his bicycle over the narrow strand that stretched to a massive blue rock in the distance. Then she sat down in her chariot. Bangs came out of the house and sat down beside Sam. With his head turned in the direction of the diminishing Thomas, Bangs said, "When the tide comes up, it covers the road to Blue Rock. Tide rises early today."

Sam looked at Bangs for a minute. Then she said, "Pardon me while I go to the moon."

Bangs stood up. He stretched his front legs. Then he stretched his back legs. Slowly he stalked away from Sam toward Blue Rock.

Suddenly Sam had no desire to go to the moon. Or any other place either. She just sat in her chariot and thought about Bangs and Thomas.

She was so busy thinking that she was unaware of thick muddy clouds that blocked out the sun. Nor did she hear the menacing rumble of thunder. She was almost knocked off the doorstep when a sudden gust of wind drove torrents of rain against her face.

Sam leaped into the house and slammed the door. She went to the window to look at Blue Rock, but she could see nothing through the grey ribbed curtain of rain. She wondered where Thomas was. She wondered where Bangs was. Sam stood there looking at nothing, trying to swallow the lump that rose in her throat.

The murky light in the room deepened to black. Sam was still at the window when her father burst into the house. Water streamed from his hat and oozed from his boots. Sam ran to him screaming, "Bangs and Thomas are out on the rock! Blue Rock! Bangs and Thomas!"

As her father turned quickly and ran out the door, he ordered Sam to stay in the house.

"And pray that the tide hasn't covered the rock!" he yelled.

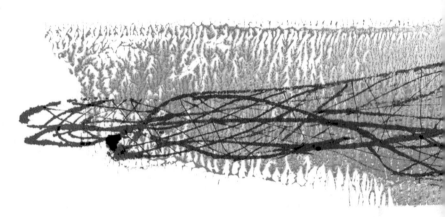

When her father had gone, Sam sat down. She listened to the rain hammer on the tin roof. Then suddenly it stopped. Sam closed her eyes and mouth, tight. She waited in the quiet room. It seemed to her that she waited forever.

At last she heard her father's footsteps outside. She flung open the door and said one word: "Bangs?"

Sam's father shook his head.

"He was washed away," he said. "But I found Thomas on the rock. I brought him back in the boat. He's home now, safe in bed. Can you tell me how all this happened?"

Sam started to explain, but sobs choked her. She cried so hard that it was a long time before her father understood everything.

Finally, Sam's father said, "Go to bed now. But before you go to sleep, Sam, tell yourself the difference between REAL and MOONSHINE."

Sam went to her room and crept into bed. With her eyes wide open she thought about REAL and MOONSHINE.

MOONSHINE was a mermaid-mother, a fierce lion, a chariot drawn by dragons, and certainly a baby kangaroo. It was all flummadiddle just as Bangs had told her. Or *had* he told her? Wouldn't her father say that a cat's talking was MOONSHINE?

REAL was no mother at all. REAL was her father and Bangs. And now there wasn't even Bangs. Tears welled up in Sam's eyes again. They ran down into her ears making a scratching noise. Sam sat up and blew her nose. The scratching was not in her ears. It was at the window. As Sam stared at the black oblong, two enormous yellow eyes appeared and stared back. Sam sprang from her bed and opened the window. There sat Bangs, his coat a sodden mess.

"Oh Bangs!" cried Sam, as she grabbed and smothered him with kisses. "What happened to you?"

In a few words Bangs told her that one moment he was on the rock with Thomas and the next he was lying at the foot of the lighthouse tower a mile away. All done by waves.

"Nasty stuff, water," Bangs grumbled, as he washed himself from his ears to his feet.

Sam patted Bangs. "Well, at least it's not flummadiddle. . . ." Sam paused. She looked up to see her father standing in the doorway.

"Look! Bangs is home!" shouted Sam.

"Hello, Bangs. What's not flummadiddle?" asked Sam's father.

"Bangs! And you! And Thomas!" answered Sam. "Oh, Daddy! I'll always know the difference between REAL and MOONSHINE now. Bangs and Thomas were almost lost because of MOONSHINE. Bangs told me."

"He *told* you?" questioned Sam's father.

"Well, he would have *if* he could talk," said Sam. Then she added sadly, "I know cats can't talk like people, but I almost believed I *did* have a baby kangaroo."

Her father looked steadily at her.

"There's good MOONSHINE and bad MOON-SHINE," he said. "The important thing is to know the difference." He kissed Sam good night and left the room.

When he had closed the door, Sam said, "You know, Bangs, I might just keep my chariot."

This time Bangs did not yawn and shake his head. Instead he licked her hand. He waited until she got into bed, then he curled up at her feet and went to sleep.

The next morning Sam opened her eyes to see an incredible thing! Hopping toward her on its hind legs was a small, elegant, large-eyed animal with a long tail like a lion's. Behind it strolled Bangs and her father.

"A baby kangaroo!" shouted Sam. "Where did you find it!"

"It is *not* a baby kangaroo," said Sam's father. "It's a gerbil. I found it on an African banana boat in the harbor."

"Now Thomas can see a baby kangaroo at last!" Sam squealed with joy.

Sam's father interrupted her. "Stop the MOON-SHINE, Sam. Call it by its REAL name. Anyway, Thomas won't come today. He's sick in bed with laryngitis. He can't even talk. Also his bicycle got lost in the storm."

Sam looked down at the gerbil. Gently she stroked its tiny head. Without raising her eyes, she said, "Daddy, do you think I should *give* the gerbil to Thomas?"

Sam's father said nothing. Bangs licked his tail.

Suddenly Sam hollered, "Come on, Bangs!"

She jumped out of bed and slipped into her shoes. As she grabbed her coat, she picked up the gerbil, and ran from the house with Bangs at her heels. Sam did not stop running until she stood at the side of Thomas' bed.

Very carefully she placed the gerbil on Thomas'
stomach. The little animal sat straight up on its
long hind legs and gazed directly at Thomas with
its immense round eyes.

"Whaaaaaaaaaaa sis name!" wheezed Thomas.

"MOONSHINE," answered Sam, as she gave
Bangs a big wide smile.

Evaline Ness needs no introduction as an admired artist of great skill and sensitivity. Her illustrations for *All in the Morning Early* by Sorche Nic Leodhas and *A Pocketful of Cricket* by Rebecca Caudill have brought these books runners-up for the Caldecott Award and have been praised for their perceptive interpretation of the author's text. This time, for SAM, BANGS, AND MOONSHINE, Miss Ness wrote the story she has illustrated.

A believer in variety, Miss Ness is always experimenting with new techniques—and has become an expert in many types of reproduction, including her own inventive methods of achieving a particular effect. She has been a highly successful commercial artist, and her illustrations have appeared in many of the leading national magazines. She has developed an interest in the art of needlework and designs and executes her own tapestries.

Miss Ness was born and grew up in Pontiac, Michigan. She studied at the Art Institute in Chicago, the Art Students' League in New York, and the Accedemia di belle Arti in Rome, Italy. She now resides in New York City.

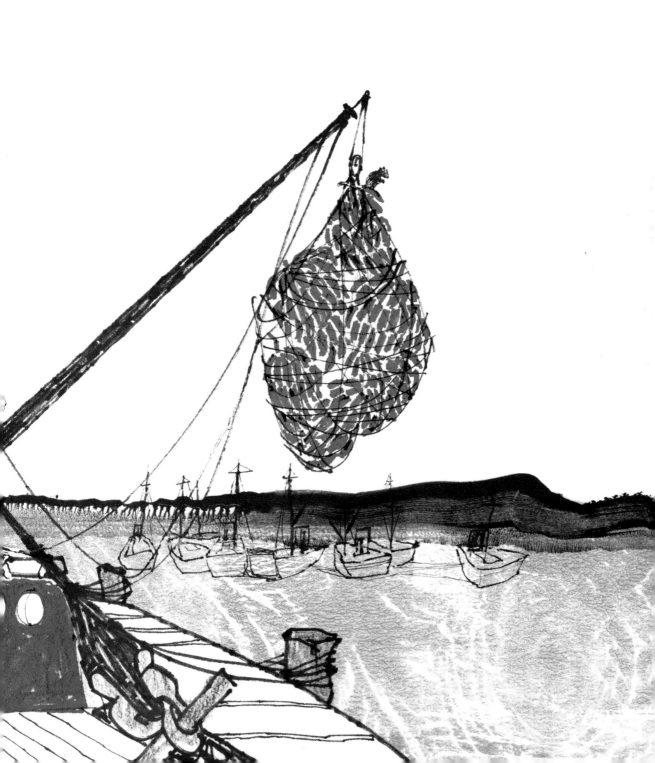